Unexpected
COMPANY

Unexpected COMPANY

Melisa Calcote

Unexpected Company

Copyright © 2024 by Melisa Calcote. All rights reserved.

No part of this publication may be reproduced, stored in a retrieval system or transmitted in any way by any means, electronic, mechanical, photocopy, recording or otherwise without the prior permission of the author except as provided by USA copyright law.

The opinions expressed by the author are not necessarily those of URLink Print and Media.

1603 Capitol Ave., Suite 310 Cheyenne, Wyoming USA 82001
1-888-980-6523 | admin@urlinkpublishing.com

URLink Print and Media is committed to excellence in the publishing industry.

Book design copyright © 2024 by URLink Print and Media. All rights reserved.

Published in the United States of America
ISBN 978-1-68486-883-4 (Paperback)
ISBN 978-1-68486-886-5 (Hardback)
ISBN 978-1-68486-885-8 (Digital)

25.03.24

He stands on top of one of the highest mountains not far from the west coast, listening to the birds flying overhead, and scanning over the horizon, looking, seeking for anything that did not look right. He is one of the Archangels that help look over humanity. As for the guardian angels, they were assigned to individuals to guide them through their lives and be there for them in any way that they can without interrupting the motions set in place for their lives. The one thing he was most definitely accurate in was noticing and sensing all distress calls from anywhere in the world, and be able to track them down within an instant. The purpose of his mission was given to him the Lord God Almighty himself. And he thinks to himself, "I wonder what I am going to come across today. I do believe I know where I might find her." As he looks up overhead, he notices an airplane full of passengers headed out over the sea towards the Caribbean islands. He scans the plane to notice that most was alright on the flight she would be on; except for this one unusual character who seemed to be on a different kind of mission. And the angel thinks to himself, "Well, maybe I better ride along to check things out. Never know what might just happen." So, he flies up toward the side of the plane was at, and invisibly goes straight through the side of the plane into the cargo bay below. He looks around to notice several dog kennels placed in the middle of the area to where the guard can keep an eye on them. They immediately sense his presence within the area, and begin barking at him. The barking sounds seemed to arouse the guard who was posted on that level of the plane.

"Ump, who's there?" the guard says startling himself, he immediately jumped up from the stool where he was sitting there close to the door. He heard the dogs barking even though he had no idea that the angel was present on the plane. He pulls his pants up and walks down the aisle towards where the kennels were stored that were placed closer to him than he was comfortable with.

"Ok guys, what do you see that I don't see?" he asked the dogs as if they were really going to answer him. As the dogs were barking in the other direction where the angel was standing, the guard then replies, "I do not see anybody. What in the world is wrong with you guys?" He asks begins walking straight through the angel. At the point of impact with the angel, he looks bewildered. He stopped and looks over his shoulder, and then turns around to see no-one there.

"Shhh." The angel whispered to the dogs, trying to quiet them down, "You'll just get him all upset." And as if there was a dog whistle being blown, the dogs stopped barking instantly

The guard looks directly at the kennels.

"No, I did not really tell you guys to shut up. I may be a security guard, but your help would be greatly appreciated too," he says as he walked toward the middle of the kennels and stopped there in front of the dogs. Scratching his, as he pulls off his cap, he looks all around the middle of the kennels, and then up into the rafters where other crates were stored. "No, I could have sworn I felt something very strange. Ya'll did not sense something unusual? Now didn't you guys see something?" he asked no-one in particular since the dogs gave no reply., "Well, fine. Don't then," he says grunting, "That's alright. I will just go back to my post," he says turning around and then says over his shoulder, "Now you just shout if you see something." The guard, Mike, takes another round through the many aisles before he decides to get settled back at his post there close to the entrance that leads to the upper deck of the plane. The angel quietly approaches the entrance door by the guard, and he proceeds through to the other side that led to the next level up, to where second-class passengers were sitting. On the other side, he looks around to the sounds of chatter among passengers as they visited with others around them. There were some visiting with new friends they just met on the plane, and as for those that would just assume be looking out the window at the puffy clouds that they were flying through. And seeing the birds at a distance watching their distance from the wingspan of the plane.

Jenny, a young woman in her late twenties, sits up close to the front of the plane, staring out the window, off in another world, and wondering to herself of the many sites she would see and the family she will see there at the islands. She knew this time would come, for she knew things had already become serious with her boyfriend, David. They had been dating now wince the year they graduated from college six years ago. He Aunt Jessie was the oldest in her mom's family, although she knew how active she has been for many years, especially since her husband died. Aunt Jessie used to come and visit every other spring in Jenny's hometown in Cheyenne, Wyoming. There were other items and interest accounts that were to be divided among her children.

"Pardon me, miss," a young man asked, "May I ask if you have any gum?" as he was trying to open his jaw trying to get his ears to pop from the rise in altitude.

"Oh yea. Sure," Jenny replies as she reaches into her bag for a stick of gum, and handing it to him, "Are you alright?"

"Oh, I will be soon. I just forgot to pick up some gum in the souvenir shop before I left the airport," he says standing there in the aisle, "I have this problem every time I fly. I just hate that. Don't you?" he asked attempting to make conversation with her.

"Oh yes," Jenny said smiling, "That is why I am always prepared for anything. Otherwise, I would probably be asking for a stiff drink."

"A drink would be nice," the young man says as he slips into the empty seat beside her.

"Yes, but actually I don't really drink," she says as she bent over to put her bag back under her seat.

"Oh, I see," he says, "I am just an occasional drinker, myself. By the way, my name is Jeffrey Haynes," he says reaching out his hand.

"Very nice to meet you, Jeffrey," she replies politely and shaking his hand, "I am Jenny Smythe. I am going to visit family. Where are you headed?" she questioned him.

"Well, I am going to see a distant cousin who was raised on the islands. Isn't it quite a beautiful place to visit?"

"Yes, it is. I have been there a few times over the years."

"Hey love, are you okay?" a young man walks up and said to her as he noticed a stranger in his seat.

"Yes, I'm okay," she said as Jeffrey quicky got up from his seat and waves bye to her and returns to his own seat, "He seems harmless," she said as he sat down beside her.

Jenny and David had been now for six years since college and he was coming back with her to meet they rest of her family. David had been planning to purpose to her while on their little excursion to the Caribbean islands, which he had been longing to do for a long time.

After retrieving their bags from the conveyer belt at the airport, they were heading out the front door, when Jenny looked over her shoulder and noticed this guy again, Jeffrey, who was right behind them. But then she noticed that he was meeting someone there in the waiting area. They approached a taxi, and the driver opened the trunk of the car and loaded their luggage into the back before getting into the car himself.

The angel was not far behind them as he hovered over the taxi.

"Where to today?" he asked as he settled into the drivers' seat and buckled up.

"The Best Western," David replied, "That's where we're going," David said sitting back and putting his arm around Jenny as she snuggled up under his arm. "Baby, I am looking forward to meeting your Aunt Jessie. Is she as adorable as you?"

"Yes, and more. She is the life of the party when she walks into the room. She can tell you who every Tom, Dick and Harry is and where all of them live on the island."

They were quiet through the drive to the hotel which took about twenty minutes including the traffic hey had to go through to get there. Just before they were about to check in, Jenny called her aunt to let her know that they had arrived and was about to check in. But when she was discussing this with her aunt about checking in at the Best Western, she said "Nothing of it, darling. Please come on out to my place. I have got plenty of room for both of you to stay during these two weeks."

"Well," Jenny said as she knew David had overheard the conversation, "I guess we're going to Aunt Jessie's."

David smiled at her, "She is family. She would not want us just staying anywhere. You should know that."

So, after they retrieved their luggage and cancelled their reservation, they grabbed another taxi and headed out to her aunt's house. Upon their arrival at the villa, they were greeted by the maidservant of the household. As they came through the front door, David was amazed to see what a grand place she had there in the Caribbean's.

"Wow! This is an awesome place! I love it," David said as he came into the front greeting room that led into the family room, where her aunt was anxiously awaiting their arrival.

"Jenny! It is so great to see you. I just cannot wait to plan our time together. How was your flight?" she asked them as she put her arms around both on each side.

"Oh, it was nice. It was quite a ride. It has been a while since I have seen you. I know you must really miss mom."

"Yes, I do miss my sister a lot. But you know, I try to stay in contact with her at least twice a month. You know what, when your family moved to Wyoming, I just was not quite adjustable for the cold weather. So, this is home to me. Charlie is out back in the stables. You will get to see him in a little bit. First, why don't we get you both settled into your room," she said as they were walking towards the stairway leading to the second floor.

"How long have you lived here now?"

"Oh honey, it has been at least thirty years since we moved here. And you know how much I miss your Uncle Joe; God rest his soul. Do you remember when he passed away ten years ago?" Aunt Jessie said leaning against a door frame to the first room to the right. "But you know what? There are so many things that keep me preoccupied here. There is so much mission work that needs to be done around here. It will take a lifetime to finish it all. And I am so happy that you came to visit."

"Thank you for inviting us," Jenny said before she opened the door to a nice size bedroom with a beautiful view of the estate.

"This is where you both will be sleeping during your stay."

"There's one thing, though," Jenny hesitated, "We'd rather have separate rooms if you don't mind."

"No problem. David can be right across the hall from you. All you must do is meet in the middle," she said smiling. "Oh, young love." Aunt Jessie said before turning around. "I will leave you both to get settled in. And then you come on down once you finish. I have got a nice little agenda for you that would give you both a fun adventure."

"Oh?" David asked picking up his luggage and turning around, "I can't wait to begin this adventure."

So, they entered their assigned quarters and commenced to unpack. Jenny went into the bathroom that was connected to her bedroom, and proceeded to unload her bathroom items. She freshened up a bit and combed out her long auburn hair. Jenny took after her mom with the curly hair and a sweet disposition. There was a swooshing of wind that went through the room as she approached the dresser. Then suddenly, she swung around to see only the furniture quiet as if nothing was there. "I could've sworn I felt something," she said to herself, "maybe it's just my imagination." At that point, the angel, Michael, was standing on the balcony of the window observing and making sure everything was alright.

Meanwhile, on the other side of town, there was a couple meeting at an outside café that was located there on a corner. Jeremy approached her, "Have you heard anything?" he questioned her as he pulled up a chair.

"No, not yet," she said opening a menu pretending to read it, "we'll get our chance," she said as she looked up and smiled at him. "And how was your ride? Any trouble along the way?"

"No. Just tried to get a little acquainted with her. She is very observant of everything. We cannot let her get on to us."

A waitress came by, "Can I take your order?" she asked in the native tongue.

Jeremy looked up, "I'll have the sweet cakes with coffee, and the same for my sweet love," he said. After she took their order, they proceeded to get down to business of their plan to kidnap Ms. Jenny

Smythe, the heir to her aunt's estate. They thought of every reason in the book of what questions that might be asked while there were in town.

After finishing that last bite of sweet cake and taking his last drink of coffee, he looks across at her.

"Well, my dear," he says taking her hands in his, "By the time we leave here, we'll be rich."

And after they said their good-byes, the both left in the same direction that they came.

As they ascended the base of the stairs, Jenny and David noticed her cousin, when suddenly, Charlie comes flying through the front door. He looks passed them into the family room to see that his mom was not sitting in her favorite chair.

"Charlie," Jenny says catching his attention, "How are you doing?"

"Doing great, Jen," he says as it was a nickname he had given her a long time ago. "It is great to see you. Have you seen mom?"

"No, just got in. I am sure that she is not far from the kitchen," she said knowing fully well that her aunt always enjoyed helping in the preparation of dinner.

"Oh yes, thanks." He says and flies off towards the kitchen. The young lad, not much younger than Jenny, had some exciting news to share. "There you are," he said coming into the kitchen as he noticed his mom up in her elbows in the middle of everything

"What is it dear?"

"Chantilly just had her third colt," he said beaming, "I am going to call the Vet over. Ok?"

"That is great! So, what is it?"

"It's a boy!" Charlie said, "This one is the one I am training for the races. You got to come see him," he says to everyone present in the room since Jenny and David had just caught up with him. Charlie, the youngest of her children, had already trained two other thoroughbreds for others to race or use as show horses. He was all excited and beside himself, like a proud father.

Later, after dinner and visiting with each other, everyone walked outside to the stables to see the new colt. Charlie was kneeling beside the colt stroking his neck when Jenny came over to see the newborn.

"So, what are you going to name him?" she asked.

"I do not know yet. Ted, the vet, says he is going to be a very strong fireball"

"That's it," she said, "Fireball!"

"Yea, that is a great name. I like that one," Charlie said beaming with joy.

"How long will it take for Chantilly to regain her strength?" his mom asked.

"Well, Ted says she will be ok after a few days. She will be good within the stall with her baby. I have got this all prepared for him. Nothing in there for him to hurt himself," Charlie said.

"I think we need to let them be for now. They both need rest and Chantilly will be ready to feed very soon since she is on her feet.

As they were leaving the stables, Jenny looked up to see a shooting star streaking across the sky.

"Wow. That is beautiful," David said admiring it, "Don't forget to make a wish."

"Oh, I just did," Jenny said smiling up at him.

When they were almost back to the house, they saw a shadow back by the stable is it disappeared into the dark,

"What was that?" Aunt Jessie asked as she pointed toward it.

"Don't' know. But I am going to go check it out," Charlie said he turned back around.

"I'll walk with you," David said following him.

The women went back into the house. When they came into the family room, Aunt Jessie settled down into her rocker as Jenny plopped down on her favorite couch nearby.

"I hope everything's okay," Jenny said.

"Oh, I'm sure it's probably nothing."

Ten minutes later, the guys came trudging into the room and made themselves comfortable in the extra-large chairs that seemed to swallow them up.

"Whatever it was had already left," Charlie said, "But I'll check again later before bedtime."

"Okay dear," Aunt Jessie says. And then they went over their agenda for the next few days.

Saturday morning, everyone all met in the family room and was anxiously waiting for the excursion that Aunt Jessie had planned for them. After piling into the Jeep that she used for getting around on the island, she drove them through the scenic route along the beach toward the opposite side of the island. They enjoyed the beautiful scenery along the way, and Aunt Jessie also pointed out to Jenny a great outlet where they could go shopping later.

Arriving at their destination, she parked the jeep not far from the beach. As Jenny was getting out, she looked around to see such a beautiful landscape draped across the waters' edge.

"I like this spot. It is very tranquil here," she said as she pulled off her sandals and threw them into the back floorboard, as did everyone else.

"Yes, and you'll soon see why I like coming here."

"Yes, I remember. I just wish Charlie was able to come," Jenny said. Charlie had stayed back at the house to look after and take care of his horses. They followed Aunt Jessie along the waters' edge a they strolled down the beach toward some tall rocks that went up to the of the mountain there close to the sea. As they waded into the shallow part of the water, they went around the front of the rocks where there was an entrance into a cave. Flying overhead was Michael, not getting too close to them. Coming into the cave, they walked along the wall of the cave, a they light from outside seemed to fade away. The water was only knee dep, as Aunt Jessie led them into a different part of the cave, further to the back. When the darkness fell upon them, she shown her flashlight up ahead to see where they were going. Then another fifty feet, it suddenly started to become brighter. Looking up, they could see where the light shown in from outside from above them. But there was something shining in the darkness that Aunt Jessie wanted to show them. There were gemstones embedded into the ceiling and walls of the cave. Jenny and David were amazed by the beauty that was all around them. They walked around looking at each of the gemstones to see what colors of the rainbow shown through the cave. The thing that Aunt Jessie warned them was that no-one was ever to take these out of the cave, for it would steal it of tis beauty.

"I wish I could bring one home with me," Jenny said eyeing the ruby gemstone in front of her.

"Oh, my dear, I do know of a place where you can acquire one just like that one," Aunt Jessie said and told her of a Souvenir store that had quite a few different sones that were found all around the island. They wandered around in the cave for the next hour admiring the stones before arriving back into the sunlight. The water shimmered with the undergrowth on the seabed. Jenny looked down to watch a turtle gliding by them along the shallow edge of the water. After coming out of the water, Aunt Jessie pulled out a blanket and the picnic basket from the jeep. She had always prepared for little trips like this for she also advised them to wear swimsuits under their clothes, so that they could really enjoy the beach. Jenny came over to the blanket and pulled off her dress. Before she knew it, David was already in the water, carrying her out to throw her into the water.

"Okay already," she said to him as he held her, "You couldn't wait to do that."

And just before getting out her last word, he threw her into the water. She came up spitting out water and eventually got him back as she chased him around in the water. They played around and swam for a while as Aunt Jessie sat at the waters' edge soaking up the sun. When it got closer to lunch, everyone came back to the blanket to calm down for a while. Looking around the beach, Jenny could see only a few other people that were walking or jogging down by the waters' edge.

David leaned over to her, "So how is it that you're the heir and not Charlie?"

"I can answer that for you," Aunt Jessie pined in. "I had already mentioned it to Charlie a while back, and he said he just wanted to have his own place. So, I did not bug him about it. But it was Charlie who wanted Jenny to have the as her own one day."

"Oh, okay. I see," David said leaning back. "Are there other caves around on the island?"

"Yes, there are. This one is the most beautiful. The others have things that you can take from the caves for yourself. I will make sure to take there later this week. But first things first," Aunt Jessie said, looking at her watch.

"So, what's next on the agenda ?" Jenny asked her aunt

"Well, let's see. There is a quaint little café we can go by that I think you would love. They serve some of the most delicious desserts."

"I'm game," David chimed in as he was dancing around trying to get his pants back on. Jenny had already put her dress on over her swimsuit. Once David heard dessert, he could not wait. They gathered up their belongings and piled into the jeep.

"Where is this place?" Jenny asked, "Did we pass it on the way out?"

"Oh, no dear, but we'll just drive toward the other side of town," she said as she backed out of the sand parking lot.

"This is a nice place. I like this," David said from the back seat as he leaned forward in between the two front seats.

"I like it here. There is always something going on."

They travelled back toward town and took a different route to the other side. The island was big that there was always some special occasion going on Jessie enjoyed the community around her. She never met a face she did not know.

As they drove up to the café on the corner, they saw several couples sitting at tables located outside the café.

The dining area inside was almost full, so they found a vacant table there close to the corner.

"May I help you?" the waitress asked as she approached their table. After looking over the menu, they gave her their orders. David went for the Ginger cakes and Jenny ordered a dessert that had chocolate in it. Aunt Jessie got her usual coffee with a slice of lemon pie. They enjoyed the scenery as they watched people either riding bicycles or on mopeds going by. Jenny was intrigued by the mopeds because they did not go that fast.

"Wish I had one of them," Jenny said, "that would be nice for getting around town at home." Then she paused for a moment, she thought that she saw Jeremy at a distance.

"What's wrong?" David asked.

"I thought I saw that guy from the airplane."

"Well, you're more than likely to see some of the other passengers from the flight also," Aunt Jessie said.

"That's true," she said picking up the napkin beside her coffee cup to dab her lips. They sat there for a while, and just before they were about to leave, Jenny excused herself to go to the ladies' room. Walking through the crowded room, she spotted the restrooms closer to the back of the café where a door that led to an alley in the back.

Just as she was coming out, this lady that was standing close by grabbed her by the arm.

"Going somewhere?" she asked as she shoved a hand gun into her ribs from behind.

"Huh? Who are you?"

"If you scream or yell, I will shoot. So, take it slow and easy if I were you," the woman said as Jenny was led out the back door into the alley.

As they were coming down the stairs into the alley, Jenny noticed several big boxes lined up against the wall stacked three boxes high. When they started walking down the side, there was Michael, who came flying by with a swoosh going past them.

"What the?" the lady said looking around.

All Jenny could think was "stay calm." Then as they came in front of more boxes stacked four boxes high, Michael shoved the boxes down onto them. Jenny broke free from the strangers' grip, and knocked her to the ground, and she took off running to the side of the building that led around to the front of the café.

"Aunt Jessie!" she said running up to them, "let's go quickly! Someone just tried to grab me," Jenny said grabbing her purse from the chair.

"Oh?" she asked. But did not hesitate, and they got into the jeep and left before the stranger made it around the corner only to see them driving off.

"UUghh!" she said almost in a growl. "This is going to be harder than we thought." And she turns around to look over her shoulder, Jeremy pulling up in a car.

"What's wrong?" he questioned with his arm hanging out the window. I thought you said this was a piece of cake." She climbed into the passenger side and gave him a dirty look.

"Let's go. There will be other opportunities to grab that witch."

"Okay dear," he said with a shrug, and drove off.

"Wow. Are you okay?" David asked Jenny with his hand on her shoulder.

"Yes, I guess. That just really scared me a bit. That woman pulled a gun on me," Jenny said finally calming down and she told them what happened.

On the way to the villa, they stopped by the dress boutique like Aunt Jessie promised. The women browsed through the store as David stayed close to Jenny. After another thirty minutes, Jenny had an armful of dresses she wanted to try on. David did not seem to mind because she came out and modeled each dress for him. He enjoyed this part, for he also remembered her taste of style in dresses. There were about four dresses he gave her the thumbs up that she liked also. By the time they checked out, both Aunt Jessie and Jenny were carrying two bags each.

"I like that blue dress especially," David said getting into the back seat at his designated spot for the ride. And the ladies handed him their bags to look after.

"It matches your eyes," he said smiling at her then gave her a peck on her cheek.

After arriving back home, all had retreated to their quarters to shower and clean up before dinner was served in the dining room. Charlie had joined them by this time. He had worked in the stalls all day cleaning a feeding the horses.

"Who knows? I sure hope not," Jenny said. "I wouldn't want to run into her again if I can't help it."

Everyone went to bed for they knew the next day of hang gliding was ahead of them. When they arrived at their destination high up on a cliff that looked out over the sea beyond with everything behind them. The instructor was there prepared for three flyers. Aunt Jessie was going to keep up with them in the jeep along the beach. After instructions were given, Joe mounted his glider and said they should follow him so that everyone lands safely. Joe had already backed up twenty to thirty feet. He too a running start and took a flying leap off the cliff as if he had done this a thousand times. And then a few seconds, he glides back up to the altitude needed where they could see him. Then each one got ready and followed the same route that Joe did. After Charlie took off, he wasn't too far behind them. As they glided along higher into the atmosphere, they could look down and see Aunt Jessie following them along the edge of the waves rushing up to the sand.

"This is fun!" Jenny yelled over to David on her right. And he nodded back to her as he was having a blast himself.

They glided out away from the beach for about a couple of miles out over the waves of the sea. Joe pointed down toward the water. Jenny gave him a questionable look, and then looked smiled to see such a delightful view of the sea life below. Everyone enjoyed the real air scenic view before Joe took a left turn that headed back toward the beach. The whole time they were in the air, there was Michael flying up high overhead them. Even Michael enjoyed the view of the most beautiful scenery below.

Not long after gliding over the beach was a clear spot where Aunt Jessie was waiting for them. Each one came in for a landing within the clearing. Jenny was the last one to land, however Michael saw something in the bushes and became concerned. Instead of Jenny landing in the clearing as planned, Michael got behind the glider and made it go a little further into the bushes where the couple was hiding. As Jenny went flying passed them, the wrings of the glider caught them off their balance when they began to get up from their position. The glider made them flip over backwards, really catching them off guard, and Jenny did not realize they were there as she was hanging on for dear life. Finally, the glider came to a slow stop within a small clearing in the trees.

"What's going on?" Jeremy said almost yelling at his companion.

"Heck if I know. One minute I'm behind the bush, the next minute, I'm being flown backwards at least five feet behind me," she said brushing herself off.

"Are you okay?" he whispered to her.

"Yeah, just fine. Let's just get out of here before they notice us," she said as they crept off away from the landing.

David came running over to Jenny to see if she was alright with the others trailing behind him.

"What happened?" Joe asked "these gliders usually don't have a mind of their own, unless there's a might wind coming."

"Well apparently it had a mind of its own this time." Jenny said out of breath. So, the others helped him get Jenny's glider back into the wide-open clearing. Joe's wife had just drove up in a four-ton truck, ready to help him load them up.

The rest of the day was uneventful with a leisurely stroll down the beach before returning to the villa. Jessie was a little worried that all this happening since they arrived. So, when she returned to her house, she retreated to her room to call someone of the law. They talked for a while before she hung up and came back downstairs to see that everyone was having pizza in the living room as they were watching a show on television. She did not say anything because she didn't want to alarm Jenny of any scare. Instead, they chatted about their adventure for the next few days. Jenny looked forward to that, because she always enjoyed a nice camping trip since her family used to go camping quite a bit when she was younger.

The following morning, everyone was preparing for the trip when Charlie came up the stairs and knocked on Jenny's door.

"Hey, everything okay? How are the horses doing?" jenny asked as she opened the door.

"They are doing fine. Matter of fact, I am going to catch up with y'all after I take care of a few things here around the stables. My neighbor will come over later to check on the horses periodically to feed and give them water."

"Oh, that's good. I would hate for you to miss out on some fun in the outdoors with us," Jenny said when David came out of his room with a backpack prepared for the next two days.

"I'm ready," he said smiling " this is going to be fun." After everyone had gotten everything together that was needed, they loaded into the jeep and headed out.

There was a place where they were going that Aunt Jessie thought would be a great place to get away from the bustle of what has been going on. She was thinking that at least Jenny did not realize of the situation.

It took them at least forty minutes to drive to the secluded part of the island where the land was fertile with trees and rose bushes in bloom along with the animals that roamed the land. They got out at a spot where Jessie parked the jeep since the forest was too thick to go through. After retrieving their gear, and carrying a cooler , they started their track.

Aunt Jessie led the way as she was the only one knowing which way to go. They followed the rugged path behind her as she pushed aside limbs and foliage up ahead. They walked through some of the thickest part of the land. As they were walking by, a snake was going the opposite way. Aunt Jessie just tiptoed way away from it. David shrugged his shoulders in a shiver, "I'm glad we got a tour guide." Jessie just smiled at him and kept going. It was obvious that she had great respect for the wildlife in the area. They also walked past rabbits that stuck their heads out to see what or who was coming long enough before going back into their burrow. They did not see any of the bigger animals.

"The cougars just assume stay to themselves unless you invade their territory," Aunt Jessie stated. David looked at her, "I thought this whole area was their stomping grounds."

"No, dear, they know where home is."

And Jenny cracked a giggle at that. It was not too much further when they came into an opening where there was a stream that flowed down from a small water fall. Jessie looked up to the top where the falls came over the rocks, "That's where we're going!"

Jenny looked around. "Why not down here?"

"The critters come out at night to enjoy the water," Aunt Jessie said.

Unexpected Company

Jenny looks around the beautiful stream, "I guess there's no going into the water here."

"That's right. Now you know why I brought plenty of water bottles."

"Okay," Jenny said, "Works for me," as David nodded in agreement.

They made their way up the side of the waterfall which was a hundred feet up; going over rocks and under tree limbs. By the time they made it to the top, they looked down from where they came. David looked down and then at Jessie.

"No wonder she's in good shape," David admits, "I would be too if I did this once or twice a week."

Jenny giggled behind him as she noticed a fish flying up into the air and over the falls.

"I'm sure we can catch fish for dinner, " she said as she threw her backpack onto a rock close by.

"I agree with that. I have got a small fishing pole with me."

"One or two?" David asked plopping down on another big rock close by.

"Don't worry. I have got two with me."

"Sounds great to me," he said as he gently laid down a two-man tent. Jenny had the other one. They set up camp about twenty feet from the water's edge. Jessie pulled out her miniature set of kitchenware for camping. She laid out a marking in the ground for the intended fire for the night. As they scouted close by for twigs and fallen small dry limbs, Jessie got other little item set out including her matches. By the time David got the fire lit, Jessie had put together the two-part fishing poles.

Jessie walked over to the waters' edge and threw her line out into the water half way towards the other side.

David picked up the other pole and said, "No worms? How are we going to catch fish without bait?"

"Just watch and learn young man," Aunt Jessie said she was eying the line in the water. Within the next few minutes, she hauled in a five-pound fish. She pulled it up, and David did not even ask. He decided not to argue with someone who obviously knew what they were doing.

Jenny pulled out bottle water, found herself a nice soft patch of grass and got comfortable as she watched them in amusement. About a half hour later, they had caught enough fish for dinner. Jessie knew that her son would be coming soon. Jenny helped her prepare the meal over the fire. Jessie had used four sticks that she stuck straight through the fish. She laid a layer of strong aluminum foil a few inches above the fire on one of the camping cookware. David went and gathered some more firewood and returned with an armful. And following not far behind him was Charlie.

"Look who I found," David said laying the wood close to the fire.

"You must've taken a different rout," Aunt Jessie said as she tended to the fish.

"Yeah, I found a different way to come. A little further the other way," as he pointed "the climb up isn't so rough."

"Hey, we could have come up that way, couldn't we? " David asked Aunt Jessie.

"Honey, it wouldn't be called hiking if you didn't have some adventure there too," she said smiling, "Now, would it?"

"Yes ma'am," he finally nodded, "After all, that's what makes it fun."

Not long after Charlie put his backpack in the tent he would be sharing with David, dinner was ready. Each one had a fish to feast on as they sat around the fire. By this time, the sun was beginning to go down. They enjoyed the sounds of the forest as they lay back on the ground after dinner. Looking up into the sky, they could see the stars beginning to shine brighter into view as they watched in awe the glorious scene around them,

David was lying next to Jenny as he reached over to grab her hand and smiled at her. She smiled back at him, "Isn't this just gorgeous?"

"Yes, it is," he said as he sat up and she also sat up beside him. David looked over at her aunt, and then back to Jenny. Jenny noticed Aunt Jessie nodding and smiling.

"Jenny," David said pulling a small box out of his front pocket.

"Yes?" she was really surprised.

As he opened the box and put a ring on her finger, "Will you marry me?" he asked. She looked at the ring in amazement and back to him.

"Yes, David. I will marry you. I Love you sweetheart," she said with tears in her eyes. At that moment he leaned forward and kissed her. Jessie did not even say a word because he had already told her of his plans. She hugged him tight and leaned into the comfort of his arms around her.

"I love you too, Jen," he said as he kissed her on her forehead. Jenny looked over at her aunt.

"How did you know? Surely you gave a drill," she said.

"Well Jenny, I had already talked to your mom because you both arrived. They already knew."

"What? Really? " She questioned and looked up at David, "You've been planning this for a while, huh?"

"Yes, and your parents gave us their blessings, after your father did give me the drill."

"I knew he would do that. He always did that with any guy who wanted to take me out on a date."

"But you chose me," he said smiling, "out of those other guys who tried to swoon you."

"Yes, I did, dear. You are the best catch of the day." she said smiling up at him.

"Oh really? Not I'm a catch!"

"Oh, come on. You know I was waiting for the right man to come along."

"Yes, I guess I'm real lucky."

"Yes, and so much more, sweetheart," she said before she kissed him again.

"Okay guys," Charlie said, "Remember, we are still sitting over here. And no, you cannot have a tent to yourselves. Rule of the house."

"By the way," David looked over to him, "Who made up that rule anyway?" Aunt Jessie was waiting for the right moment when she knew that was coming eventually in any of their lives ass they were growing up.

Melisa Calcote

"Well, you know. I do believe it all started a very long time ago," Aunt Jessie said putting her hand on her chin.

"Huh?!?" asked all three of them

"It started with an ancestor of the family. He always believed it was the right thing to do."

"Now you know it's totally different these days," David chimed in, "most couples in the present would move in together first before they even get to Home base"

"You are right, David. But we're not most people, are we?"

David was sitting straight up by this time when Jenny said, "No, we are not. Are we David? We both decided this together. Remember?
"

"Oh yes, I remember very well," David said half way smiling, "I would hate to be in a debate with your aunt. She drives a hard bargain." After that comment, everyone cracked up laughing at his answer.

Suddenly, they heard someone screaming at a distance as it sounded like they were running in the opposite direction away from campsite.

"That sounded like two people scream," Jenny said looking over her shoulder" I wonder what happened."

"It sounds like the cougars ran them out of their territory," Charlie said chuckling.

On the other end of the forest from where they came were a couple who were trying to outrun the cougar as they jumped over bushes and hightailed it out of the forest as fast as their feet could carry them. As they got closer their vehicle, the cougar ad already given off the chase. It was the other highlight of the evening. Jeremy and his lady friend had gotten into the car; made sure the windows were up and locked the doors. They sat there panting and catching their breath. She looked over at him.

"Another brilliant idea he said," she said glaring at him.

"Alright. Alright." He said patting her shoulder, "We're alive, aren't we?"

"Yes, by the skin of our hide. You know they had to have heard us." She reached down to the floor board and grabbed her drink and practically drank it all down. She handed it over to him with maybe a few swallows left. He looked at the drink and at her.

"Okay, I get the picture," he said before drinking what was left in the bottle. He put on his seat belt as she was still fuming.

"I swear I'm going to strangle you," she said shaking her hands towards him. She finally buckled up.

"Come on dear. Please calm down," He backed up and began to turn around as he saw a bright light in the sky coming down towards them. Before he had a chance to say anything else, he put the car in drive and peeled out as they were both screaming again…

Michael came down toward the ground as his light grew dimmer and laughing at them as they drove out of sight. Then Michael noticed in a distance another pair of headlights that seemed to be slowly following behind them.

"Good for them. Maybe someone caught onto their little scheme," he said smiling. Then he looked up. "I know…At least it put a scare into them. Right?" he said to the Almighty.

"Do you think it might work? You never know with people these days. Seems like a lot of things don't scare them." And it became quiet as Michael seemed to be listening to Him. Michael stood there quietly looking up into the heavens.

"Yes, I agree. That just might work."

But meantime, he did not have to worry about those two for a while, so the others could enjoy nature without any interruptions.

Back at the fireside, Aunt Jessie gave Charlie a funny look.

"Did you bring trouble with your?"

"Oh no, not me. If there was anyone following me, they would really have to be fast on their feet," he said smiling.

"Good. Now I have got some good stories to share of the past and enjoying the time together. Even though they didn't share a tent, David did get his 'good night' kiss before heading for his sleeping bag. The one thing that woke the guys up in the morning was the aroma of coffee brewing over the fire that was relit by Aunt Jessie.

"Rise and shine," they heard as she was humming a tune as she went about getting a few items out of her food bag. Everyone got a pack of their favorite pop tarts that were just a good cold, especially with a cup of coffee. Afterwards, they went out for a stroll up the stream to see where it took them. They crossed over to the other sider where a tree had fallen across the stream. David was right behind Jenny as they crossed over. She stopped halfway across and almost lost her balance. But when she felt David's hands on her hips, she regained it and kept going. The day was very nice as there was a slight breeze that kept them cool. They came up to some berry bushes when Aunt Jessie stopped to pick some for later. David grabbed a few to nibble on along the way. She pointed out some of the trees that had been there forever. When they finally came to the end of the trail, they were standing up on a high cliff that looked out over the ocean. Jenny pulled out her camera and took a few pictures and Aunt Jessie took a picture of them with the ocean behind them. As they looked down from the cliff, they could see the rocks down below with the water splashing up against the walls of the cliff. Aunt Jessie pulled the bottled water and passed it out to them and they sat down on the rocks to enjoy the sight.

"So, sweetie," Aunt Jessie said, "when do you think y'all will start planning for the wedding day?"

"Pretty soon," David said, "I'd like to have a group meeting with our parents to sort of see what everyone's schedule looks like within the next six months and your thoughts also." He said looking over at Jenny.

"Well, dear, that all depends on how soon you want to set the date," she said smiling.

"That soon?" he asked with a shocking look, "You're not going to let this fish get away, are you?"

"That's right since we have known each other for so long. Why wait?"

"Well, I guess we'll call them when we get back and see," he said since they did not bring their cell phones with them. Michael was close by as he heard them talking. Michael looked up listening to advice, as He always had good ideas and nodded. The following morning, they wrapped things up at the camp site and made sure the fire was completely out before they left to return to where the jeep was parked at the edge of the forest.

Upon their return at the house, Charlie went out to check on his pride and joy, Fireball and Chantilly. He found his friend in the stables putting out some food for them.

"So how was your camping trip?" he asked when he saw Charlie approaching.

"It was okay," Charlie said as he stroked Chantilly's nose. She was nibbling at his fingers as it was a "Good to see you" sign from her.

"David proposed to Jenny the night before."

"Hey that's great."

"Yeah, he is cool and funny. He will fit right in with our crazy family," Charlie said with a grin.

Once David and Jenny came in the door, they both went straight to get their cell phones and called their parents to find out more about their schedule for the near future. David overheard Jenny talking to her mom as she also had her on the speaker phone.

"Yes, mom. That's right. We want to get married as soon as it's possible. So, what do you think? David's parents think it is a pretty good idea, and mentioned that it might be a great idea to come here to Aunt Jessie's for the wedding It's a very nice setting for a wedding."

"Sweetheart, you just want the immediate family? Or anyone else who would like to come?"

"Well, that depends on if they could come by next Thursday. Aunt Jessie said she knew exactly who we could talk to get all the necessary papers in a snap. She has got all the right connections here, you know."

"Yes, I already know that. That is why I always called her the 'Go getter.' Remember?"

And Jenny agreed that was also true to her form.

"Jenny, let me get back to you this afternoon, so we can set up the plane reservations. And you do what you can do on that end. Okay dear?"

"Okay!" Jenny said with excitement in her voice. When she hung up with her mom, she turned around and gave David a big hug and kiss. They were very happy that things just might work out for the wedding to happen there at Aunt Jessie's villa. Jenny and Aunt Jessie started making calls to different friends and family that could also help for the special occasion.

David decided to stay out of the way, and concentrate on where he might acquire a nice tuxedo, or suit.

It was later in the day after noon; there came Jeremy snooping around the horse stalls. His lady friend, Gina, did not come with him this time. She had too much excitement within the last few days. He opened the stall to where Fireball was nibbling on a piece of carrot that was left behind for him. As Jeremy came closer, Fireball began to get skittish. He did not know this character because he had not seen him before. But as he approached the filly, suddenly, Fireball let out a sound that could wake the dead. Jeremy started backing up. "Ok, little dude, I'm not going to hurt you. Just make you disappear, if possible." He said to himself.

Fireball had somehow managed back Jeremy into the corner of his stall. With a nudge of his nose, he prodded Jeremy on his chest as if he was letting him know that he was not welcome there.

"Hey! Wait a minute," Jeremy said talking to the horse, "You got me at a disadvantage here." But Fireball kept nudging at him.

Chantilly was watching over her filly from over the rail of the stall. Fireball let out another yell. Chantilly had reached over the short wall between her and Fireball and totally knocked Jerey off his feet.

And as he landed in some horse manure, he let out an unstifled yell himself.

"Oh great!" he said as he realized what he had landed in, "Just what I needed."

Michael had entered the barn to notice what just happened, and he began laughing and the horses responded with him as they were neighing and laughing in their own language that probably got everyone's attention from the house by now. At this time, Jeremy thought he heard someone laughing. When he looked up, he noticed Michael on the other side of the stall. Then Jeremy looked like he had just seen a ghost as Michael said to him, "Don't you have anything better to do with your time?"

All Jeremy could do was give him a crazy look, and then he started to yell himself as he was really shaken up by his appearance. Michael had chosen to let himself be seen this time to Jeremy. He moved a little closer to reach out to help him up. Jeremy was hesitant about reaching out to him because Michael was not actually all there in form. But Michael said to him, "Come on, I don't bite." Jeremy slowly reached up and grabbed his hand and was surprised that he could actually touch him. He slowly rose up out of the horse manure.

"You better watch out who you tangle with. They do bite." Michael said smiling at him.

"Oh really? Someone could have told me that," Jeremy said stuttering," But but. How? Who are you? And what are you?"

Michael helped him out of the stall as Jeremy to get the smelly stuff off his pants, knowing fully well he must have smelled like a horse.

"My name is Michael, and I'm an Archangel," he said as Jeremy gave him a funny look.

"What??" he asked as he was shocked at his answer, "oh boy, I'm in trouble now."

"Jeremy, you have got some explaining to do when they arrive here. I hope it is a good one."

"Well, uh I .How the heck do you know my name?"

"Everyone upstairs knows your name. You have been a trouble maker since you were a teenager. You know, you did not have to follow in your father's footsteps."

"Why do you think I did that? I was trying to get attention, and it only got me into trouble every time. I really wanted them to know who I really am. I was a very lonely child," Jeremy said still brushing off stuff, "But how can I make it right now? They will not believe me."

"It's easier than you think, but you've got to make the first step," Michael said as he gave a questionable look. Michael started to turn around to leave when Jeremy said "Hey! I have got to do this by myself?"

"Jeremy, you are not by yourself. Believe in yourself for once and trust people around you. Just remember that. I will still be here for you. Believe me, she will understand," Michael said before he faded into the scenery around him.

Just as Jeremy started wiping his pants again, the whole family showed up as they came walking into the barn. As Aunt Jessie got closer, she recognized him.

"Jeremy Leonard! What are you up to?" Aunt Jessie asked when she came closer.

"Umm. Hi Aunt Jessie," he said almost stuttering. She walked over to him and gave him a hug even though he stunk to high heaven.

"Aunt Jessie?" Jenny asked when she saw Jeremy. "What is really going on here?" she asked Jeremy, "Are we re related?"

"Yes, Jen. We are related," Jeremy said stepping back because of the smell, to explain. But Aunt Jessie answered instead.

"Jenny, Jeremy is my nephew from my husband's side of the family, and he's also your brother."

"What? How?" Jenny looked confused and bewildered.

"He is the first born in your family. Jeremy is seven years older than you," she said as Jeremy gave a slight frown, "When he was born, your mom was not able to take care of him because she was too young. His father did not even stick around to man up to his own responsibility. My sister, Ella, adopted him so he would still be a part of our family."

"Whoa! Incredible!" David said, "This is getting interesting."

"Yea, you think?" Jenny asked, and then turned to Aunt Jessie."But how come mom never told me?"

"Well, that's partially because she was ashamed to admit I came from a broken family and from a raunchy and a no-good father," Jeremy said still working on his pants "So in essence, I should've been the first to inherit Aunt Jessie's fabulous estate here."

Jessie gave him a surprised look and began to wonder. It was a very awkward moment. Then Jeremy broke the silence.

"Hey, do you think it's possible if I can get out these yucky pants?" And everyone starting laughing that broke the tense situation between them. They all went back to the house. Charlie gave him a pair of his pants to change into, even though they were a little baggy for Jeremy. He changed his pants and handed the smelly ones over to the housemaid, who was holding her nose as she walked off with them with two fingers.

He met them in the family room, as he overheard Jenny and Aunt Jessie discussing something.

"I guess I'm in trouble now," he said finding an empty chair to tall into. Jessie turned to him

"No, you are not in trouble. Rightfully, you are the first born of the family," she said smiling.

"So, what are you smiling about?"

"Well, you know this place is big enough for both of you to share," as she noticed Jeremy's face went from a frown into a smile.

"For real?"

"Yes, for real," she said as she felt someone's hand on her shoulder, and she looked over her shoulder but no-one was there. She could imagine that it could have been her late husband there in their presence. Michael was on the other side of the room standing by Jeremy, trying to reassure him as he had his hand on Jeremy's shoulder. Jeremy felt a shiver run up his spine as he felt Michael's touch.

"You know my husband, Joe would not have it any other way, than to see this place filled with lots of love and laughter of family once again. So, Jeremy, your persistence paid off." By this time, Jenny and David were beaming because they were excited also. Jenny had already talked with her mom about everything. And Jenny was not even upset about the present situation. Jenny was thinking to herself, "At least now, I do have a brother to pick on, and look forward to getting to know him better. I am looking forward to this new venture."

"I have a proposition for you both," Aunt Jessie said and all were on the edge of their seats in anticipation. "After your wedding here, Jenny and David, I would just love for you to come live here. And you too, Jeremy. There are lots of job opportunities here on the island and the other islands close by." Jeremy was once and already pleased with the outcome.

And Aunt Jessie turned to Jeremy, "And Jeremy, I really want to make this right for you. So, if you will agree to be able to be a loving and supportive brother, you can also stay here. For you both have a lot of catching to do," she said as they both look at each other.

"Yes, I agree. You have got that right. We do have a lot to catch up on. I look forward to sharing everything with my sister, Jen." He said as his smile got broader.

"Since I still live here, you both will have to share the responsibilities of the household here." She said as both of them were nodding. "Jeremy, since you're the oldest, your role is to make sure to keep this place immaculate and kept up. You already know how I take pride in having a place where anyone can come. You can also help Charlie with the horses."

"That sounds like fun," Jeremy said, "So long as Fireball doesn't try to corner me again."

Everyone laughed at his antics as Jenny noticed that he was also a clown at heart, and he enjoyed making people laugh. That was a quality that grew in their family.

"Jenny, you can be over the kitchen personnel, even though I know you'll also want to work with others within the community."

"Oh you know I do. I could get a job working with the special education children and others on the islands. I would certainly enjoy that," Jenny said.

The next couple of days, everyone spent time on preparing and getting everything ready for Jenny's wedding to David. Saturday morning, David rode into town with Jeremy to a men's clothing store to browse through the suits on the sale rack. One was at one rack browsing as Jeremy was at the other.

"So tell me Jeremy. Wasn't it hard growing up in the other family and not being able to see your mom or Jen?"

"Yes, it was very hard. Well, mom, Ella, told me when I was around seven that I was adopted. And they told me who my real mom was. I guess that's a good thing though."

"How do you figure that?"

"Well, most other children never find out or ever get to know their real parents," Jeremy said.

"That's true. At least now you can spend as much time as you want with Jenny,"

Unexpected Company

"For real dud." Jeremy was shocked at his reply.

"Yes, really. She is your sister. I would never hear the end of it if Jenny wasn't able to at least spend time getting to know you."

For a quick awkward moment, the guys had a special moment as David just reached over and gave him a pat on the back. And then they went back to their shopping. Another hour later, they did walk out the door with a suit for the special occasion .

Arriving back home at Aunt Jessie's , the guys came back to an empty house. "Looks like we've got the whole place to ourselves," David said as they looked around the first floor as he was looking to see if anyone was there.

"What? No note?" Jeremy said walking into the kitchen and to see if by chance there was a note left on the refrigerator.

"Doesn't look like it."

David went upstairs to pick up his suit and see if Jenny was in her room, and came trotting back down the stairs.

"Not there either," he said coming into the family room.

"Well, I know what I need to do, write my 'Love' message for the ceremony," he said as he picked up a pad and pen that was on the coffee table.

"Well, guess we'll see what good movie is on the tube," Jeremy said as he picked up the remote.

"Sounds good to me, maybe it'll give me some ideas for this," he said flipping the pen back and forth in between his fingers.

As Jeremy flipped through the channels, the guys actually found an old movie that they both wanted to see again. They talked about their future and plans for different things they decided was worth holding true to. Especially spending more time with family and Jeremy being able to spend time with his real mother. Jeremy got up and took a walk out onto the front porch that stretched across the main house. The one thing Aunt Jessie brought with her when they moved to the island was definitely the idea of having a porch across the front. And a swing and lounge chairs to sit and enjoy the breeze from the o"Whcean that seemed to fill the air with a sweet smell of the ocean. Jeremy walked over and sat down on the swing, when he realized that he was not by himself, he looked around to see Michael right behind him.

"Oh my God! Don't scare me like that dude! You could scare the wits out of someone," Jeremy said catching his breath.

"So how are things going?" Michael asked.

"Seems to be going pretty good. I know you're not just here for me, are you?"

"You're right. But I'd like to make sure you don't sneak out of this."

"Oh, no way. Since things are out in the open now and Aunt Jessie isn't too upset with me, I'm grateful for that. Things can finally be set right for our family. Don't you think?"

"Yes, that's true. I'm very happy for you and Jenny. Just do one thing, and everything will fall into place for you."

"What's that?"

"Don't leave the scene when you think things seem to get tough."

"Okay. I think I can do that," he said thinking, "Do you know something I don't know? Is Jenny's or my mom's health in jeopardy?"

"No, Jeremy. But it could happen real soon, and we can't stop it from happening. So whatever happens in the future, stay strong for your family if you truly love them. They're the only family you have. Cherish that.".

"Okay, I think I see what you're saying," he said as he turned around and then Michael was gone. "Oh man!"

Very soon he went back into the house to finish watching the movie with David. When the others got home, they came into the family room to see two grown mean crying, wiping their eyes. "What're y'all watching?" Aunt Jessie asked when she noticed their reaction.

"Gone with the wind," David said, "That is such a touching movie," he said as he dabbed his eyes with the back of his hand.

"No wonder! I would be crying to by the end of this movie. I can't believe you both actually like that movie."

"Yes, it's one of the all-time favorites in best movies as far as I'm concerned," Jeremy said drying his eyes.

"Wow, at least I know we've got two sensitive men in our family," Jenny said smiling.

"Honey, I'm going to lie down and rest a bit," Aunt Jessie said, "I'm a little bushed," she said before give Jenny a peck on her cheek and going upstairs.

"Okay. I might just go for a walk," she said when David got up from the couch to join her.

"I'll go with you, hon. I need to get out and stretch my legs. Do you want to come Jeremy?"

"No man. I'm good. See you guys when you return," he said before retreating back to the overstuffed chair. He picked up the pad where David had started writing his vows to Jenny and browsed through what he had already written. "Pretty good," he said to himself, "so long as you make my sister happy, then I'm happy." After thirty minutes passed by, Jeremy thought he heard something upstairs, and for sure he did hear a faint cry. So he ran up the stairs two at a time, down , he knew something was wrong.

"What is it? Is it your heart?"

When all she could do was shake her head, he called the doctor on the island and the local hospital. However he also knew exactly where the hospital was on the opposite side of the island. He decided it was a better idea to get her into his car and bring her to the hospital himself. It took him maybe ten minutes to pick up His Aunt and bring her down to his car that was parked close to the door. Once he got her into the back seat, she was still conscious. And he laid her at an angle on the back seat with a couch pillow under her head.

"Don't worry. I'm going to take you there myself. If I pass them on the way, then they'll have to come in their car. Okay?"

She nodded, and within a minute, he was already behind the wheel buckled up, and put the car into drive. As he was driving down the road, he saw Jenny and David walking back.

He pulled over and said "Get in quick. It's her heart."

They didn't argue and David got into the front seat with Jeremy as Jenny crawled in the back seat with her aunt, and put her hand on Aunt Jessie's lap.

"Aunt Jessie, it's okay. We'll get you there as fast as we can." Jeremy knew all of the shortcuts through all the streets to get to the hospital, and he went in a zig zag direction as the streets were like a puzzle. But he got them there within record time of twenty minutes and even passed the ambulance. When they saw him, he waved at them, and they turned around and followed him back toward the hospital.

Once everyone got there, the paramedics piled out and got Aunt Jessie onto a gurney and straight into the emergency room, where her doctor was waiting impatiently as he was pacing back and forth preparing instruments for this emergency.

As soon as she was escorted and prepped for emergency surgery, the family was escorted to the waiting room, and Jeremy went and parked his car and ran back in.

"God, I hope we got here in time," Jeremy said to the others.

"Me too," Jenny said, "I need to call Charlie to let him know what happened. I'm not quite sure where he's at right now. But I know he's got his cell phone with him."

She dialed his number and soon as he picked up, Jenny brought him up to date of all of what just happened. After she hung up, she walked over to a coffee station and poured herself some coffee, and offered David and Jeremy some. But they didn't have the desire for any. Not long after, Charlie showed up. Two hours went by before they knew it, and still no word from the doctor or the nurse. Then Jenny got up and was walking down the hall toward the emergency room to see if she could find out anything. Not long after arriving by the emergency room door, the doctor came out into the hall. He walked back with her to the waiting room. He came a little closer to them.

"Guys, I'm sorry," he said sadly, "I tried everything humanly possible to save her. Your Aunt has been quite a joy to know and be with through these thirty years. She was quite the caring lady of the community. I'm going to miss our friendship. But I have a feeling she's where she want to be now. She's with Greg."

Jenny broke down in tears as David and the doctor tried to comfort her. Doctor Gunn came closer to Jenny and wrapped his arms around her, as Jessie was a close friend of his for a long time. He knew how much she would be missed. Jeremy was sitting down at the time beside Charlie, when he knew Charlie had to been hurting pretty bad also; when he gradually put his arm around him to try to console him. Charlie seemed almost frozen as if he couldn't believe it.

"Wow! Charlie? Talk to me man. Are you okay?" Jeremy asked him as he squeezed his shoulder. Then it seem like Charlie was giving in to his own emotions.

"Why now? Why?" was all he could get out at the moment. Jenny came over to them, even though she was crying, and they all came together as a group holding each other in a circle, shoulder to shoulder, and they came together as family and prayed for strength.

Charlie finally let it out later when he saw Jenny calling her mom and dad. He was pacing around the room with Jeremy not far behind him. After a while, Jenny came over to Charlie and just held him. He really needed that gentle touch of her hug.

"Don't worry, Charlie. We'll get through this. And we'll help with whatever needs to be done, okay?" and he looked up and nodded to her. Jeremy was just as upset as anyone else there, and had to restrain himself from doing exactly what Michael had said to do. So he walked down to the chapel on the same floor of the hospital for some quiet time. When he was walking down the aisle, he realized that David was right behind him. They sat down on the first pew.

"If only I hadn't done the stupid things I've done," Jeremy said, "Maybe this wouldn't have happened."

"Jeremy, don't beat yourself up over this. This is not your fault. Sometimes stuff just happens that we can't control. You know that. Right?"

"I guess, but man, it just hurts," Jeremy said as he pounded his chest, "She was as strong as an ox. I just don't understand."

"Nobody does. Sometimes it just happens, and no one can do anything about it. Because we're only human. Remember?"

Jeremy look at him as if he had already heard those same words earlier in the day. And they sat there in silence as they both prayed for strength for their family.

Within the next couple of days, Jenny's parents and Charlie's brother and sister and they family showed up at the house. And by the afternoon, more of the family came to be them as they helped them complete the funeral arrangements. The funeral was that Wednesday morning at a graveside ceremony where they all met to say their good-byes to one of the liveliest members of their family. Jenny was standing by her mom with David on the other side. And David and Jeremy wore their suits for the first time, even though that's not exactly how they planned it. Someone from the church sang "Amazing Grace", which was one of Aunt Jessie's favorite songs followed by "The Band Played on" as she used to call it the going out song. It was Charlie's idea to play that song because he knew that's what she would've wanted. Not long after the funeral was over, everyone returned to the house, where members of the church had already brought different dishes and casseroles for the family. During the whole time, Michael was close by for the comfort of the family, as he always did.

Jeremy was standing outside when Charlie, his brother Robert; his sister, Julia; and David and Jenny came over to him. He saw them coming and thought he knew what was coming.

"What's up?" Jeremy asked as they approached him.

"Jeremy," Charlie said, "just don't let me down, and we're cool. Remember, you are part of our crazy family, whether you like it or not. And Jeremy smiled at that.

"Yea, don't worry about it. All that's happened has really made a big change in my life. I Love you guys," Jeremy finally was able to say to them. And they came together as one.

Two days later, arrangements were still on for their wedding. The family stayed for the special occasion as it was something very special to them. The family room had been transformed into a chapel setting with candle stands at the front to the left, where do podium stood. The room was filling up fast with friends and family that wanted to be there for them. Although two days ago, they were grieving the loss of Aunt Jessie, they also knew that Aunt Jessie always said "Let the Band play on. Be blessed and live life to the fullest. For only the heavenly father knew when He would bring you into the other world where peace and joy shined on forever!"

At the reception, the band played some of Aunt Jessie's favorite music, as "Yes" she was the life of the party. And the last song that the band played was a favorite of the family. It was "They'll know We are Christians by our Love." We are One in the Spirit, and One in the Lord. One big family.

www.ingramcontent.com/pod-product-compliance
Lightning Source LLC
LaVergne TN
LVHW021743060526
838200LV00052B/3448